Manx Cats

BY TAMMY GAGNE

The Child's World®

Published by The Child's World®
1980 Lookout Drive • Mankato, MN 56003-1705
800-599-READ • www.childsworld.com

Acknowledgments
The Child's World®: Mary Berendes, Publishing Director
Red Line Editorial: Editorial direction
The Design Lab: Design
Amnet: Production
Design elements: iStockphoto; Africa Studio/Shutterstock Images;
Willem Havenaar/Shutterstock Images

Photographs ©: Yann Arthus-Bertrand/Corbis, cover, 1, 10, 23;
iStockphoto, cover, 1, 7; Africa Studio/Shutterstock Images,
cover, 1; Willem Havenaar/Shutterstock Images, cover, 1;
Photos.com/Thinkstock, 5; Selmer Hess/Public Domain, 9;
Shutterstock Images, 13, 21; Cheryl Kunde/Shutterstock Images,
15; David Gilder/Shutterstock Images, 17; Cynthia Baldauf/
iStockphoto, 19

ISBN 9781626873834
LCCN 2014930625

Printed in the United States of America
Mankato, MN
July, 2014
PA02226

ABOUT THE AUTHOR

Tammy Gagne has written dozens of books about the health and behavior of animals for both adults and children. Her most recent titles include Great Predators: Crocodiles *and* Super Smart Animals: Dolphins. *She lives in northern New England with her husband, son, and a menagerie of pets.*

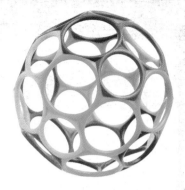

CONTENTS

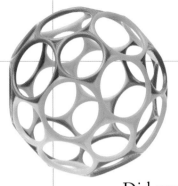

A Well-Rounded Cat

Did you know there is a cat **breed** without a tail? It is called the Manx cat. This popular breed has been around since ancient times. It is loved for its spirit and its special look.

Some Manx cats have tails. Their tails may be so short people can barely see them. Or they may be a little shorter than other cats' tails.

Manx are known for their heavy look. Nearly every feature is round. The head, eyes, and even the bottom are round. Manx cat's front legs are shorter than their back legs. This adds to the cat's heavy appearance.

Manx are playful cats. They enjoy running and jumping. Many people say Manx act more like dogs than cats. Some members of this breed even enjoy playing **fetch**. Manx get along with children, making them great family pets.

Most Manx cats are born without a tail, giving them a special look.

Cat Tales

The Manx breed began on the Isle of Man. This tiny island is in the Irish Sea. It lies between Great Britain and Northern Ireland. Scandinavian Vikings entered the island in the 700s. They brought longhaired cats with them. These cats mated with the shorthaired cats already on the island.

Stories about Manx cats have been passed around for years. One story suggests that crossing a cat and a rabbit created the breed. Another story claims the Vikings stole cats. They believed their tails were good luck.

Another story says mother cats bit their kittens' tails off. This made the kittens less appealing to the Vikings. Both stories are interesting. But neither story is true.

Over time a change in the cats' genes occurred. This change caused some kittens to be born with short tails. Some kittens had no tail at all. The gene that created kittens with no tail was strong. Soon many kittens were born without tails.

The first Manx cats came from the Isle of Man in Europe.

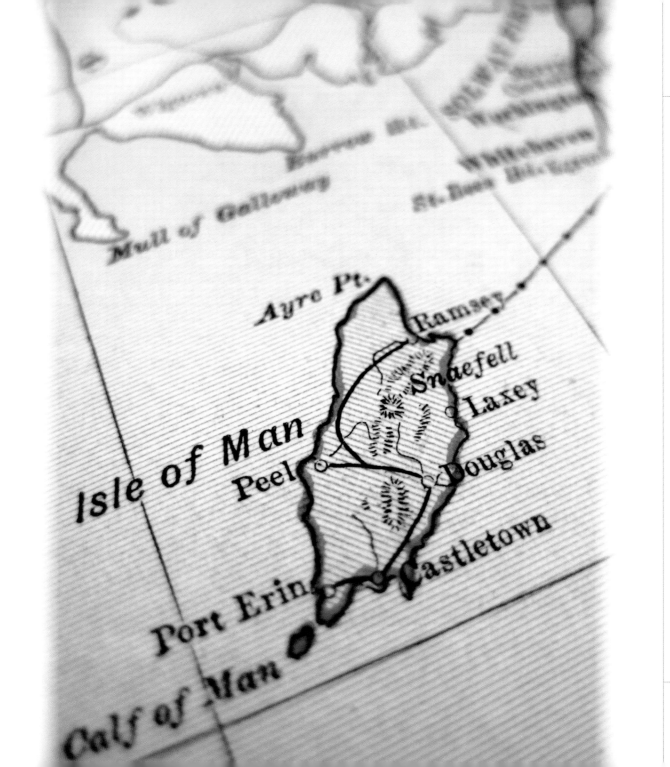

Now Showing

The Manx continued breeding on the Isle of Man. The island is removed from land. No new cat breeds were brought to the island. This helped the Manx breed stay the same.

Manx also had a strong gene for short hair. But some Manx were born with long hair. This came from the Vikings' cats.

People have been showing Manx in professional cat shows since the 1800s. Longhaired Manx were not popular until later. The Manx breed has been around longer than The Cat Fanciers' Association (CFA). This is the world's largest cat **registry**. The CFA was founded in 1906. The Manx was one of the first breeds accepted.

A Manx with no tail is called a rumpy. Manx with the beginning of a tail are called rumpy risers. A rumpy or

The longhaired Manx is called the Cymric. It has all the same features of a Manx. It simply has a longer coat.

a rumpy riser can compete in CFA show championship classes. Manx with tails can compete in the "all other varieties" class.

Manx cats have appeared in books and cat shows since the 1800s.

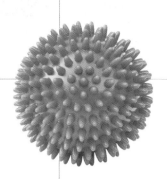

Pretty and Powerful

The Manx is more than the cat without a tail. This breed is prized for its round features. Manx cats are medium in size. Adult males weigh between 10 and 12 pounds (4 and 5 kg). Females weigh between 8 and 10 pounds (3 and 4 kg).

One feature that makes Manx cats look rounder and heavier is their fur. Shorthaired Manx have a thick, double coat. They have a soft undercoat. But their topcoat is rough and shiny. Longhaired Manx have a soft and silky coat. All Manx cats have neck **ruff**. They also have fluffy fur on their legs.

The Manx's front legs are much shorter than its back legs. This makes the cat look more round. Its bottom is higher than its shoulders. Some people wonder if the Manx has good balance. Other cat breeds use their tails for balance. Their tails help them when running and jumping. The Manx's powerful bottom keeps it steady instead. Manx are known for being skilled runners and jumpers.

Manx are powerful cats that can jump very well.

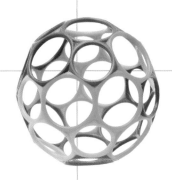

The Long and the Short of It

Manx come in a wide range of colors and patterns. These include white, **tabby**, and black and white. Tortoiseshell Manx have black hair. It is mixed with shades of red.

When a female Manx has kittens, their tail lengths vary. A single litter can include kittens with tails and kittens without them. Some kittens may also have longer tails than others.

Many people only want to own rumpy or rumpy riser kittens. The high demand has led some breeders to **dock** tailed cats. This means they shorten the tail through surgery. Other people believe this is hurtful to the kittens.

Manx are called kittens for one year. The breed grows slowly. Many Manx are not fully grown until they are five years old.

Nearly all tortoiseshell cats are female.

Some Manx cats have a tabby coat.

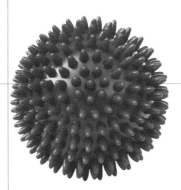

A Fierce Companion

Manx cats enjoy playtime. They also enjoy family and playing with humans. Manx can be very active. But they can also be calm and loving.

Manx bond closely with their owners. They also get along great with other cats and dogs. They do not need another animal as a companion. But Manx cats do not like being left alone for long periods. It may be a good idea to have another animal if you are away a lot.

Manx kittens learn to hunt right away. They practice hunting with toys or bugs. Manx cannot live with pet **rodents**. They will hurt or kill them. If any unwanted rodents appear, Manx will use their hunting skills.

Manx cats are very loyal. This breed has a strong **instinct** to protect. Manx are known to act as guard cats.

Manx cats are good hunters and enjoy being outside.

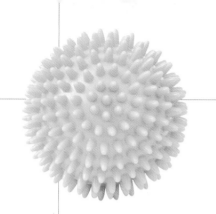

Cat Burglars

Manx cats are interested in water. But this doesn't mean they want to be in it. A Manx may walk around the edge of a full bathtub. It may bat at the bubbles with its paws. But if it slips into the water, the Manx will not be happy.

Manx cats have a special talent for opening doors. This may not be surprising. Many cats slip their paws under doors to pull them open. But Manx do not use this common trick. They often figure out how to turn door handles.

Manx are not loud like some cat breeds. They purr and meow softly. They also make another sound. It is called a **trill**. It sounds like the Manx is singing. Female Manx cats make this sound to call their kittens. Manx also trill to get their owners' attention.

Because Manx are such good jumpers, they can get into the highest cabinets.

Although Manx cats do not enjoy being in the water, it is important to bathe them.

All a Big Game

Manx love to play chase. They will usually be the one to start the game. They may even want other pets to play. It is unlikely that a bigger animal, such as a dog, will win. The Manx is known for its speed and swiftness.

If you do not have other pets, buy your Manx toys to chase instead. They like puzzle toys that give out treats. Laser pointers, balls, and toy mice are also great choices.

Manx enjoy learning. Most are very smart. Owners can teach Manx cats simple commands. This is another way they are like dogs. Teaching tricks is a good way to keep your Manx active.

The Manx has an odd walk for a cat. It hops like a rabbit. This is because of its short front legs.

Manx are playful cats. They may even hide in grocery bags!

Handle with Care

Manx are usually healthy cats. They can live into their teens. But owners must provide a certain amount of care. This helps them stay happy and healthy.

Take your Manx for a yearly checkup with a veterinarian. They will check your Manx and keep it healthy.

Another important part of good care is grooming. Brush your Manx once or twice each week. This removes dead hair. Manx will shed the most in the spring and fall. You should brush more often at these times.

Be careful of your Manx's bottom. This area can be sensitive. Be gentle when holding your cat. Be sure to support the bottom properly. Simply letting the cat's bottom dangle can be painful for them.

A healthy diet is important to the Manx's health. The breed loves food and becomes overweight quickly if owners aren't careful.

It is important to take good care of your Manx so it can live a healthy life.

Glossary

breed (BREED) A breed is a group of animals that are different from related members of its species. The Manx is one type of cat breed.

dock (DOK) To dock is to cut short. Some Manx breeders dock cat's tails.

fetch (FECH) To fetch is to go after and bring back. Manx cats enjoy playing fetch.

genes (JEENS) Genes are the parts of cells that control the appearance, growth, and other features of a living thing. Over time, the genes in some cats changed to create the Manx.

instinct (IN-stingkt) Instinct is a natural ability. Manx have a strong instinct to protect.

registry (REG-uh-stree) A registry is a place where official records are kept. The CFA is the world's largest cat registry.

rodents (ROHD-uhnts) Rodents are small mammals that have sharp front teeth used for gnawing. Manx hunt for rodents.

ruff (RUHF) Ruff is a fringe of long hairs or feathers growing around or on the neck of an animal. All Manx cats have neck ruff.

tabby (TAB-ee) A tabby is a cat with a striped or spotted coat. Some Manx have tabby coats.

trill (TRILL) A trill is a quick high sound that is repeated. Manx cats trill to get their owners' attention.

veterinarian (vet-ur-uh-NER-ee-uhn) A veterinarian is a doctor who treats animals. It is important to take your Manx to the veterinarian.

To Learn More

BOOKS

Bailey, Gwen. *What Is My Cat Thinking?*
San Diego: Thunder Bay Press, 2010.

Gagne, Tammy. *Amazing Cat Facts and Trivia*.
New York: Chartwell Books, Inc., 2011.

WEB SITES

Visit our Web site for links about Manx cats:
www.childsworld.com/links

Note to Parents, Teachers, and Librarians: We routinely verify our Web links to make sure they are safe and active sites. So encourage your readers to check them out!

Index